little Miss Scatterbrain

by Roger Hargreaves

Little Miss Scatterbrain was just a little bit forgetful.

You can say that again!

Little Miss Scatterbrain was just a little bit forgetful.

She met Mr Funny.

"Hello Miss Scatterbrain," he said.

"Hello Mr Bump," she replied.

She met Mr Tickle.

"Hello Miss Scatterbrain," he said.

"Hello Mr Strong," she replied.

She met Mr Happy.

"Where are you off to?" he asked her.

She thought.

And thought.

"I bet you've forgotten, haven't you?" laughed Mr Happy.

Little Miss Scatterbrain looked at him.

"Forgotten what?" she said.

Miss Scatterbrain lived in the middle of a wood.

In Buttercup Cottage.

Everybody knew it was called Buttercup Cottage.

Except the owner.

She kept forgetting.

I know," she thought to herself. "To help me remember, I'll put up a sign!"

Look what the sign says.

She isn't called Little Miss Scatterbrain
for nothing

Is she?

One winter's morning, she got up and went downstairs to make breakfast.

She shook some cornflakes out of a packet.

But, being such a scatterbrain, she forgot to put a bowl underneath.

"Now, where did I put the milk?" she asked herself.

It took her ten minutes to find it.

In the oven!

After breakfast she set off to town.

Shopping.

She went to the bank first.

"Good morning Miss Scatterbrain," smiled the bank manager.

"What can I do for you?"

Little Miss Scatterbrain looked at him.

"I'd like some..."

"Money?" suggested the bank manager.

"Sausages!" replied Miss Scatterbrain.

"Sausages?" exclaimed the manager. "But this isn't the butcher's. This is the bank!"

"Oh silly me," laughed Little Miss Scatterbrain.

"Of course it is. I was forgetting."

She smiled. "I sometimes do you know."

"Really?" said the bank manager.

"I'd like two please," she said.

"Pounds?" asked the manager.

"Pounds!" agreed Little Miss Scatterbrain.

The bank manager passed two pound notes over the counter.

Little Miss Scatterbrain looked at them.

"What are these?" she said.

"Two pounds," he replied.

"Two pounds?" she said.

"They don't look much like two pounds of sausages to me!"

Eventually the bank manager managed to explain, and off went Little Miss Scatterbrain, to the butcher.

"Phew!" remarked the bank manager.

Little Miss Scatterbrain walked into the butcher's shop.

"Good morning," said Percy Pork, the butcher.

"Good morning Mr Beef," she replied.

"Pork!" said the butcher.

"No!" she said.

"Sausages!"

"But my name isn't 'Sausages'!" he said.

"Of course it isn't," she replied.

"That's what I'm here for!"

"Oh!" said Percy, scratching his head.

"What sort?"

"What do you suggest?" she asked.

"Beef?" he asked.

"I thought you said your name was 'Pork'?" she said.

Percy Pork sighed a deep sigh.

"Call me Percy," he said.

Eventually, after a little more confusion, Little Miss Scatterbrain managed to buy her two pounds of beef sausages.

Percy Pork wrapped them up for her.

"Looks like snow," he said conversationally, looking out of his shop window.

"Really?" said Little Miss Scatterbrain, looking at the brown paper parcel.

"What a funny man!" she thought to herself.

"Looks like snow indeed! Looks more like wrapped-up sausages to me!"

"Goodbye," said Percy Pork.

"Goodnight," she replied, and went out to catch a bus home.

Little Miss Scatterbrain stood behind Mr Silly in the queue at the bus stop.

Along came Mr Nosey.

He stood behind her in the queue.

He looked up at the sky.

"Looks like snow!" he remarked.

Little Miss Scatterbrain looked at the brown paper parcel in her hand.

And said nothing!

3 Great Offers for MR. MEN Fans!

MR. MEN TOKEN

1 New Mr. Men or Little Miss Library Bus Presentation Cases

A brand new stronger, roomier school bus library box, with sturdy carrying handle and stay-closed fasteners.
The full colour, wipe-clean boxes make a great home for your full collection.
They're just £5.99 inc P&P and free bookmark!

☐ MR. MEN ☐ LITTLE MISS (please tick and order overleaf)

2 Door Hangers and Posters

In every Mr. Men and Little Miss book like this one, you will find a special token. Collect 6 tokens and we will send you a brilliant Mr. Men or Little Miss poster and a Mr. Men or Little Miss double sided full colour bedroom door hanger of your choice. Simply tick your choice in the list and tape a 50p coin for your two items to this page.

PLEASE STICK YOUR 50P COIN HERE

Door Hangers (please tick)
☐ Mr. Nosey & Mr. Muddle
☐ Mr. Slow & Mr. Busy
☐ Mr Messy & Mr. Quiet
☐ Mr. Perfect & Mr. Forgetful
☐ Little Miss Fun & Little Miss Late
☐ Little Miss Helpful & Little Miss Tidy
☐ Little Miss Busy & Little Miss Brainy
☐ Little Miss Star & Little Miss Fun

Posters (please tick)
☐ MR.MEN
☐ LITTLE MISS

3 Sixteen Beautiful Fridge Magnets – any 2 for £2.00! inc.P&P

They're very special collector's items!
Simply tick your first and second* choices from the list below
of any 2 characters!

1st Choice

- [ ] Mr. Happy
- [ ] Mr. Lazy
- [ ] Mr. Topsy-Turvy
- [x] Mr. Bounce
- [ ] Mr. Bump
- [ ] Mr. Small
- [ ] Mr. Snow
- [ ] Mr. Wrong
- [ ] Mr. Daydream
- [x] Mr. Tickle
- [ ] Mr. Greedy
- [ ] Mr. Funny
- [ ] Little Miss Giggles
- [x] Little Miss Splendid
- [ ] Little Miss Naughty
- [x] Little Miss Sunshine

2nd Choice

- [ ] Mr. Happy
- [x] Mr. Lazy
- [x] Mr. Topsy-Turvy
- [x] Mr. Bounce
- [ ] Mr. Bump
- [ ] Mr. Small
- [ ] Mr. Snow
- [ ] Mr. Wrong
- [ ] Mr. Daydream
- [x] Mr. Tickle
- [ ] Mr. Greedy
- [x] Mr. Funny
- [x] Little Miss Giggles
- [x] Little Miss Splendid
- [x] Little Miss Naughty
- [x] Little Miss Sunshine

*Only in case your first choice is out of stock.

--- TO BE COMPLETED BY AN ADULT ---

**To apply for any of these great offers, ask an adult to complete the coupon below and send it with
the appropriate payment and tokens, if needed, to MR. MEN CLASSIC OFFER, PO BOX 715, HORSHAM RH12 5WG**

- [ ] Please send ____ Mr. Men Library case(s) and/or ____ Little Miss Library case(s) at £5.99 each inc P&P
- [ ] Please send a poster and door hanger as selected overleaf. I enclose six tokens plus a 50p coin for P&P
- [ ] Please send me ____ pair(s) of Mr. Men/Little Miss fridge magnets, as selected above at £2.00 inc P&P

Fan's Name _____

Address _____

_____ **Postcode** _____

Date of Birth _____

Name of Parent/Guardian _____

Total amount enclosed £ _____

- [ ] **I enclose a cheque/postal order payable to Egmont Books Limited**
- [ ] **Please charge my MasterCard/Visa/Amex/Switch or Delta account** (delete as appropriate)

| | | | | | | | | | | | | | | | | Card Number

Expiry date ___/___   **Signature** _____

Please allow 28 days for delivery. Offer is only available while stocks last. We reserve the right to change the terms
of this offer at any time and we offer a 14 day money back guarantee. This does not affect your statutory rights.
Data Protection Act: If you do not wish to receive other similar offers from us or companies we recommend, please
tick this box [ ]. Offers apply to UK only.

MR.MEN   LITTLE MISS
Mr. Men and Little Miss™ & ©Mrs. Roger Hargreaves

CUT ALONG DOTTED LINE AND RETURN THIS WHOLE PAGE